7 770436 91

D1381332

Envy

SANDRA BROWN

Envy

PIATKUS

Copyright © 2001 by Sandra Brown Management, Ltd.

First published in Great Britain in 2001 by
Judy Piatkus (Publishers) Ltd
5 Windmill Street, London W1T 2JA
email: info@piatkus.co.uk

First published in the United States in 2000
by Warner Books

The moral right of the author has been asserted

A catalogue record for this book is available from the British Library

ISBN 0 7499 0580 8

Printed and bound in Great Britain by
Mackays of Chatham plc, Chatham, Kent

Envy

Saltines and sardines. Staples of his diet. Add a chunk of rat
cheese and a Kosher dill spear and you had yourself the four
basic food groups. There simply wasn't any finer fare.

That was the unshakable opinion of Hatch Walker, who had
a sun-baked, wind-scoured visage that only a mother gargoyle
could love. As he munched his supper, eyes that had blinked
against the sting of countless squalls squinted narrowly on the
horizon.

He was on the lookout for the lightning flashes that would
signal an approaching storm. There was still no sign of it here
onshore, but it was out there somewhere, gathering energy,
sucking moisture up from the sea that it would send back to
earth in the form of wind-driven rain.

But later. Above the harbor, a quarter moon hung in a clear
sky. Stars defied the neon glare on the ground. But Hatch
wasn't fooled. He could feel impending meteorological change
in his bones before the barometer dropped. He could smell a
storm even before clouds appeared or a sail caught the first

strong gust of wind. His weather forecasts were rarely wrong. There'd be rain before dawn.

His nicotine-stained teeth crunched into his pickle, and he savored the garlicky brine, which he chased with a bite of cheese. It just didn't get any better. He couldn't figure out folks who were willing to pay a week's wages on a meal that wouldn't fill a thimble, when they could eat just as good—and to his mind a hell of a lot better—on a buck and a half. Tops.

Of course, they were paying for more than the groceries. They were financing the parking valets, and the starched white tablecloths, and the waiters with rings in their ears and cobs up their butts, who acted like you were putting them out if you asked them to fetch you an extra helping of bread. They were paying for the fancy French name slapped on a filet of fish that used to be called the catch-of-the-day. He'd seen pretentious outfits like that in ports all over the world. A few had even cropped up here in Key West, and those he scorned most of all.

This being a weeknight, the streets were relatively quiet. Tourist season was on the wane. *Thank the good Lord for small favors,* Hatch thought as he swigged at his can of Pepsi and belched around a harrumph of scorn for tourists in general and those who flocked to Key West in particular.

They descended by the thousands each year, slathered in sunscreen that smelled like monkey barf, toting camera equipment, and dragging along whining kids who'd rather be up in Orlando being dazzled by Disney's man-made marvels than watching one of the most spectacular sunsets on the planet.

Hatch had nothing but contempt for these fools who worked themselves into early coronaries for fifty weeks a year so that for the remaining two they could work doubly hard at having a good time. Even more bewildering to him was that they were willing to pay out their soft, pale asses for the privilege.

Unfortunately, his livelihood depended on them. And for Hatch that represented a moral dilemma. He despised the tourists' invasion, but he couldn't have made a living without it.

Walker's Marine Charters and Rentals got a share of the

money the vacationers spent during their noisy occupation of his town. He equipped them with scuba and snorkeling gear, leased them boats, and took them on deep-sea fishing expeditions so they could return to shore and have their grinning, sunburned mugs photographed with a noble fish, who was probably more affronted by the asinine picture-taking than by being caught.

Business wasn't exactly thriving tonight, but the trade-out was that it was quiet. Peaceful, you might say. And that wasn't a bad thing. Not by a long shot. Not compared to life aboard merchant ships, where quarters were noisy and cramped and privacy was nonexistent. He'd had a bellyful of that, thank you. Give Hatch Walker solitude and quiet anytime.

The water in the marina was as still as a lake. Shore lights were mirrored on the surface with hardly a waver. Occasionally a mast would creak aboard a sailboat or he'd hear a telephone ringing on one of the yachts. Sometimes a note or two of music or several beats of percussion would waft from one of the waterfront nightclubs. Traffic created an incessant swish. Otherwise it was quiet, and, even though it meant a lean week financially speaking, Hatch preferred it this way.

Tonight he might have closed up shop and gone home early, except for that one boat he had out. He'd leased the twenty-five-footer to some kids, if you could rightly call twenty-somethings kids. Compared to him they were. Two men, one woman, which in Hatch's estimation was a volatile combination under any circumstances.

The kids were tan and lean, attractive and self-assured to the point of cockiness. Hatch figured that between the three of them they probably hadn't done an honest day's work in their lives. They were locals, or at least permanent transplants. He'd seen them around.

They were already half lit when they boarded the craft just before sunset, and they'd carried a couple of ice chests on board with them. Heavy as anchors, by the way they were lugging them. Odds were good that those chests contained bottles of booze. They had no fishing gear. They were going off-shore strictly for a few hours of drinking and debauchery or his name wasn't Hatch Walker. He had debated whether or not to lease a craft to them, but his near-empty till served to persuade him that they were not flat-out drunk.

He'd sternly ordered them not to drink while operating his boat. They flashed him smiles as insincere as a diamond dealer's and assured him that such wasn't their intention. One bowed at the waist and could barely contain his laughter over what he must have considered a lecture from a grizzled old fart. The other saluted him crisply and said, "Aye, aye, sir!"

As Hatch helped the young woman into the boat, he hoped to hell she knew what she was in for. But he figured she did. He'd seen her around, too. Lots of times. With lots of men. An eye patch would have covered more skin than her bikini bottom, and Hatch would have no right to call himself a man if he hadn't noticed that she might just as well not have bothered wearing the top.

And she didn't for long.

Before they were even out of the marina, one of the men snatched off her top and waved it above his head like a victory banner. Her attempts to get it back turned into a game of slap-and-tickle.

Watching this as the boat had chugged out of the marina, Hatch had shaken his head and counted himself lucky that he'd never had a daughter with a virtue to protect.

Finally one last sardine remained in the tin. Hatch pinched it out of the oil, laid it diagonally across a saltine, added the last bite of pickle and sliver of cheese, doused it real good with Tabasco, stacked another cracker on top, and put the whole thing in his mouth, then dusted the crumbs off his beard.

Chewing with contentment, he happened to glance toward the entrance of the harbor. What he saw caused the sandwich to stick in his throat. The corner of a cracker scratched his esophagus as he forced it down, muttering, "Hell does he think he's doin'?"

No sooner had Hatch spoken his thought aloud than a long blast from the approaching boat's horn nearly knocked him off his stool.

He would have come off it anyway. Because by the time the intact sardine sandwich hit his stomach, Hatch was out the door of the weather-beaten shack that housed his charter service and angrily lumbering down the quay, waving his arms and shouting at the boat's pilot—probably a tourist from one of those square, landlocked states who'd never seen a body of water bigger than a watering trough—that he was coming into the marina way too fast, that he was violating the "no wake" rule, and that his recklessness would cost him a whopping fine if not a couple nights in jail.

Then Hatch recognized the boat as his. His! The damn fool was abusing his boat, the finest and biggest in his fleet!

Hatch fired a volley of expletives, wicked holdovers from his years as a merchant marine. When he got his hands on those kids, they'd regret the day their daddies spawned them. He might be old and ugly and bent, he might have gray whiskers and a slight limp from an unfortunate run-in with a knife-wielding Cuban, but he could hold his own with a couple of pretty beach boys—"And make no mistake about that, you arrogant little fuckers!"

Even after the boat cleared the buoys it didn't slow down. It kept coming. It missed a forty-two-foot sailboat by inches and set it to rocking. A dinghy slammed into the side of a multimillion-dollar yacht, and the folks sipping nightcaps on the yacht's polished deck rushed to the rail and shouted down at the careless mariner.

Hatch shook his fist at the young man at the wheel. The drunken fool was steering straight for the pier, kamikazelike, when he suddenly cut the engine and spun the wheel sharply to port. The outboard sent up a rooster tail of spume.

Hatch had barely a second to leap out of the way before the boat crashed into the quay. The young man clambered down the steps of the cockpit and across the slippery deck, leaped onto the aggregate pier, tripped over a cleat, then crawled a few feet forward on all fours.

Hatch bore down on him, grabbed him by the shoulders, and flipped him over as he would a fish he was about to gut. In fact, if he'd had his filleting knife in hand, he might have slit the guy from gonads to gullet before he could stop himself. Luckily he was armed only with a litany of curses, threats, and accusations.

But they sputtered and died before they were spoken.

Up till then Hatch's focus had been on his boat, on the recklessness and speed with which it had been steered into the marina. He hadn't paid much attention to the young man piloting her.

Now he saw that the boy's face was bloody. His left eye was swollen practically shut. His T-shirt was in shreds, clinging to his lean torso like a wet rag.

"Help me. God, oh, God." He threw Hatch's hand off his shoulder and scrambled to his feet. "They're out there," he said, frantically motioning toward the open sea. "They're in the ocean. I couldn't find them. They . . . they . . ."

Hatch had witnessed a man get shark-bit once. He had managed to pull him from the water before the shark could get more than his left leg. He was alive but in bad shape, in shock, scared shitless, blubbering and making no sense as he bled buckets into the sand.

Hatch recognized the same level of wild panic in this young man's eyes. This was no prank, no showing off, no drunken escapade, as he'd originally thought. The kid—the one who'd smartly saluted him earlier—was in distress to the point of hysteria.

"Calm down, sonny." Hatch took him by the shoulders and shook him slightly. "What happened out yonder? Where are your friends at?"

The young man covered his face with hands that, Hatch no-

ticed, were also bloody and bruised. He sobbed uncontrollably.
"In the water."

"Overboard?"

"Yeah. Oh, God. Oh, Jesus."

"That asshole nearly wrecked my yacht! What the fuck was
he doing?"

A man wearing flip-flops came slapping up, hands on hips,
reeking of a cologne that any self-respecting whore would
think was too strong. He was wearing only a Speedo swimsuit
beneath an overhanging belly covered with black curly hair. He
had a thick gold bracelet on his right wrist and spoke with a
nasally northeastern accent—just the kind that never failed to
get on Hatch's fighting side.

"The boy's hurt. There's been an accident."

"Accident my ass. He put a big dent in the *Dinky Doo.*"
They'd been joined by the man's female companion, who was
dressed in a bikini and a pair of high heels. Her tan and tits
were store-bought. Under each arm she was holding a toy poo-
dle. The pets had pink ribbons tied to their ears and were yap-
ping in angry synchronization.

"Call 911," Hatch said.

"I want to know what this son of a bitch intends to do—"

"Call 911!"

The interior of Hatch's "office" smelled of sardines, damp hemp,
dead fish, and motor oil. It was uncomfortably warm and stuffy
inside, as though the shack couldn't provide enough oxygen for
three men because it was usually occupied only by one.

The limited floor space was crowded with trunks of fishing
and diving gear, coils of rope, maps and charts, maintenance
supplies and equipment, a vintage metal file cabinet in which
Hatch rarely filed anything, and his desk, which had been sal-
vaged from a shipwreck and bought at auction for thirty
dollars.

The kid who'd crashed his boat had heaved twice into his

toilet, but Hatch figured the nausea was more from nerves and fear than from the shot of brandy he'd sneaked him when no one was looking.

Of course, the kid had had a lot to drink prior to the brandy, and that wasn't just an assumption. He'd admitted as much to the Coast Guard officer who was currently questioning him. Key West police had had their turn at interrogating him about crashing the boat into the marina. He was then turned over to the Coast Guard officer, who wanted to know what had happened onboard that had caused his two companions to wind up in the Atlantic.

He'd provided their names and ages, their local addresses. Hatch had checked the information against the rental agreement the two young men had filled out before embarking. He confirmed the data to the officer.

Hatch resented having to share his private space with strangers, but he was glad he hadn't been asked to wait outside while the laws interrogated the kid. The marina was now swarming with onlookers who'd been drawn to the scene of the drama like flies to a pile of manure. And you couldn't swing a dead cat without hitting some breed of uniformed personnel.

Having intimate knowledge of jails in numerous ports on several continents, Hatch had an aversion to uniforms and badges. He would just as soon avoid authority of any kind. If a man couldn't live by his own set of rules, his own sense of right and wrong, what was the good of living? That attitude had landed him in paddy wagons all over the globe, but that was his philosophy and he was sticking to it.

But, in all fairness, Hatch had to hand it to the Coast Guard officials and local policemen who'd questioned the young man and organized a search-and-rescue party: They hadn't been assholes about it.

It was clear that the kid was on the brink of total breakdown. The badges had been savvy enough to realize he might crack if they applied too much additional pressure, and then where would they be? In order to calm him down and get answers, they'd gone pretty soft on him.

He was still wearing wet swim trunks and sneakers that leaked seawater onto the rough plank flooring whenever he moved his feet. In addition to giving him the brandy, Hatch had thrown a blanket over him, but he'd since discarded it, along with his tattered T-shirt.

Outside, running footsteps and an excited voice brought the kid's head up. He looked hopefully toward the door.

But the footsteps ran past without stopping. The officer, who'd had his back turned while helping himself to Hatch's coffeepot, came around and correctly read the kid's expression. "You'll know something as soon as we do, son."

"They've got to be alive." His voice sounded like someone who'd been outyelling a storm for a long time. Every now and then it would crack over a word. "I think I just couldn't find them in the dark. It was so damned dark out there." His eyes bounced back and forth between Hatch and the officer. "But I didn't hear them. I called and called, but . . . Why weren't they answering me? Or calling out for help? Unless they . . ." He was unable to say out loud what they all feared.

The officer returned to Hatch's stool, which he'd placed near the chair in which the boy sat with his shoulders hunched forward. For several weighty minutes, the officer did nothing but sip his hot coffee. *Schwoop. Schwoop.*

It was irritating as hell, but Hatch remained quiet. This was the law's business now, not his. His boat was insured. There'd be paperwork out the wazoo, and a suspicious, seersucker-suited adjuster to haggle with, but in the long run, he would come out okay. Maybe even a little better off than he'd been.

He was less optimistic about how this kid would fare. No amount of insurance was going to make his life easier after this. As for the two who'd gone into the water, Hatch didn't hold out much hope. The percentages were stacked against them.

He had known a few men who had foundered and lived to tell

about it, but not many. If you went into the water, drowning was probably the most merciful way to die. Exposure took longer. And to predators you were just another source of food.

The Coast Guard officer cradled the chipped coffee mug between his palms and swirled the contents. "How come you didn't use the radio to call for help?"

"I did. I mean, I tried. I couldn't get it to work."

The officer stared into his swirling coffee. "Coupla other boats heard your SOS. Tried to tell you to stay right where you were. You didn't."

"I didn't hear them. I guess . . ." Here he glanced across at Hatch. "I guess I didn't pay much attention when he was showing us how to operate the radio."

"Costly mistake."

"Yes, sir."

"Fair to say you're not a seasoned sailor?"

"Seasoned? No, sir. But this is the first time I've had any trouble."

"Uh-huh. Tell me about the fight."

"Fight?"

This drew a frown from the officer. "Don't bullshit me now, son. Your eye's all but swollen shut. You've got a bloody nose and busted lip. Your knuckles are scraped and bruised. I know what a fistfight looks like, okay? So don't play games with me."

The young man's shoulders began to shake. His eyes streamed, but he didn't even bother trying to stem the tears or to wipe his dripping nose.

"Was it over the girl?" the officer asked in a gentler voice. "Mr. Walker here says she was a looker. A party girl, best he could tell. She belong to one of you?"

"Like a girlfriend, you mean? No, sir. She's just a casual friend."

"You and your buddy fight over her favors?"

"No, sir. Not . . . not exactly. What I mean is, she wasn't the reason it started."

"Then what was?"

The boy sniffed but remained mute.

"Just as well tell me now," the officer said, "because when we find whatever we're going to find out there, we'll keep hounding you until we get the truth of it."

"We were drunk."

"Uh-huh."

"And . . . and . . ." The kid raised his head, looked over at Hatch, then back at the officer, and said earnestly, "He's my best friend."

"All right. So what happened?"

He licked mucus off his upper lip. "He got mad. Mad as hell. I've never seen him like that."

"Like what?"

"Crazy. Violent. Like he snapped or something."

"Snapped."

"Yes, sir."

"What'd you do to piss him off, cause him to snap?"

"Nothing! One minute he's down below with her. I gave them some privacy, you know?"

"For sex? They were having sex?"

"Yeah. I mean, really going at it, having fun. Next minute, he's back up on deck, coming at me."

"For no reason? Just like that?"

The kid's head wobbled up and down. "It was supposed to be a party. A celebration. I don't understand how it went to hell so quick. I swear to God I don't." He lowered his battered face into his hands and began to sob again.

The officer looked over at Hatch as though for consultation. Hatch stared back at him, wanting to ask what he was looking at him for. He wasn't a counselor. He wasn't a parent. He for damn sure wasn't an officer in the Coast Guard or a cop. This was no longer his problem.

When he failed to volunteer anything, the officer asked if he had anything to add to the boy's story.

"No."

"Did you see or hear them fighting?"

"The only thing I saw them doing was enjoying themselves."

The officer turned back to the young man. "Best friends don't fight for no reason. Not even when they've had too much to drink. They might swap some harsh words, maybe throw a punch or two. But once it blows over, it's over, right?"

"I guess," he replied sullenly.

"So I want you to come clean with me now. Okay? You listening? What brought on the fight?"

The kid struggled to swallow. "He just attacked me."

"How come?"

"All I did was defend myself. I swear," he blubbered. "I didn't want to fight him. It was a party."

"Why'd he attack you?"

He shook his head.

"Now, that's not true, is it, son? You know why he attacked you. So tell me. What caused your best friend to get mad enough to start beating up on you?"

Silence stretched out for about twenty seconds, then the kid mumbled a single word.

Hatch wasn't sure he'd heard correctly, mainly because the first clap of thunder from the predicted storm rattled the small square window in his shack just as the boy spoke, and also because what he thought he heard the boy say was a strange answer to the question.

The officer must have thought so, too. He shook his head with misapprehension and leaned forward to hear better. "Come again? Speak up, son."

The young man raised his head and took a swipe at his nose with the back of his hand. He cleared his throat. He blinked the officer into focus with his one functioning eye.

"Envy," he said gruffly. "That's what this is all about. Envy."

P.M.E.
St. Anne Island, Georgia
February 2002

B ut there's got to be." Maris Matherly-Reed impatiently tapped her pencil against the notepad upon which she had doodled a series of triangles and a chain of loops. Below those she'd rough-sketched an idea for a book jacket.

"P.M.E., correct?"

"Correct."

"I'm sorry, ma'am, there's no such listing. I double-checked."

The idea for the book jacket—an autobiographical account of the author's murky relationship with her stepsibling—had come to Maris while she was waiting for the directory assistance operator to locate the telephone number. A call that should have taken no more than a few seconds had stretched into several minutes.

"You don't have a listing for P.M.E. in this area code?"

"In any area code," the operator replied. "I've accessed the entire U.S."

"Maybe it's a business listing, not a residential."

"I checked both."

"Could it be an unlisted number?"

"It would appear with that designation. I don't have anything under those initials, period. If you had a last name—"

"But I don't."

"Then I'm sorry."

"Thank you for trying."

Frustrated, Maris reconsidered her sketch, then scribbled over it. She wasn't going to like that book no matter what the jacket looked like. The incestuous overtones made her uncomfortable, and she was afraid a large number of readers would share her uneasiness.

But the editor to whom the manuscript had been submitted felt strongly about buying it. The subject matter guaranteed author appearances on TV and radio talk shows, write-ups in magazines, probably a movie-of-the-week option. Even if the reviews were poor, the book's subject matter was titillating enough to generate sales in large numbers. The other decision makers in the hardcover division of Matherly Press had agreed with the editor when she pled her case, so Maris had deferred to the majority. They owed her one.

Which brought her back to the prologue of *Envy* she had read that afternoon. She had discovered it among a stack of unsolicited manuscripts. They had been occupying a shelf in her office for months, collecting dust until that unspecified day when her schedule permitted her to scan them before sending the anxious authors the standard rejection letter. Imagining their crushing disappointment when they read that impersonal and transparent kiss-off, she felt that each writer deserved at least a few minutes of her time.

And there was always that outside, one-in-a-million, once-in-a-blue-moon chance that the next Steinbeck or Faulkner or Hemingway would be mined from the slush pile. That, of course, was every book editor's pipe dream.

Maris would settle for finding a bestseller. These twelve pages of prologue had definite promise. They had excited Maris more than anything she had read recently, even material from her portfolio of published authors, and certainly more than anything she'd read from fledgling novelists.

It had piqued her curiosity, as a prologue or first chapter should. She was hooked, eager to know more, anxious to read the rest of the story. Had the rest of the story been written? she wondered. Or at least outlined? Was this the author's first attempt at fiction writing? Had he or she written in another genre? What were his/her credentials? Did he/she have any credentials?

There was nothing to indicate the writer's gender, although her gut feeling said male. Hatch Walker's internal dialogue rang true to his salty character and read like the language in which a man would think. The narrative was in keeping with the old sailor's poetic, though warped, soul.

But the pages had been sent by someone totally inexperienced and untutored on how to submit a manuscript to a prospective publisher. All the standard rules had been broken. An SASE for return mailing hadn't been enclosed. It lacked a cover letter of introduction. There was no phone number, street address, post office box, or e-mail address. Only those three initials and the name of an island that Maris had never heard of. How did the writer hope to sell his manuscript if he couldn't be contacted?

She noticed that the postmark on the mailing envelope was four months old. If the author had submitted the prologue to several publishers simultaneously, it might have already been bought. All the more reason to locate the writer as soon as possible. She was either wasting her time or she was on to something with potential. Whichever, she needed to know sooner rather than later.

"You're not ready?"

Noah appeared in her open office door wearing his Armani tuxedo. Maris said, "My, don't you look handsome." Glancing at her desk clock, she realized she had lost all track of time and that she was, indeed, running late. Raking her fingers through her hair, she gave a short, self-deprecating laugh. "I, on the other hand, am going to require some major renovation."

Her husband of twenty-two months closed the door behind

him and advanced into her corner office. He tossed a trade magazine onto her desk, then moved behind her chair and began massaging her neck and shoulders, which he knew were the gathering spots for her tension and fatigue. "Tough day?"

"Not all that bad, actually. Only one meeting this afternoon. Mostly I've used today to clear some space in here." She gestured toward the pile of rejected manuscripts awaiting removal.

"You've been reading the stuff in your slush pile? Maris, really," he chided lightly. "Why bother? It's a Matherly Press policy not to buy anything that isn't submitted by an agent."

"That's the official company line, but since I'm a Matherly, I can bend the rules if I wish."

"I'm married to an anarchist," he teased, bending down to kiss the side of her neck. "But if you're planning an insurrection, couldn't your cause be something that streamlines our operation, instead of one that consumes the valuable time of our publisher and senior vice president?"

"What an off-putting title," she remarked with a slight shudder. "Makes me sound like a frump who smells of throat lozenges and wears sensible shoes."

Noah laughed. "It makes you sound powerful, which you are. And awfully busy, which you are."

"You failed to mention smart and sexy."

"Those are givens. Stop trying to change the subject. Why bother with the slush pile when even our most junior editors don't?"

"Because my father taught me to honor anyone who attempted to write. Even if the individual's talent is limited, his effort alone deserves some consideration."

"Far be it from me to dispute the venerable Daniel Matherly."

Despite Noah's mild reproof, Maris intended to continue the practice of going through the slush pile. Even if it was a time-consuming and unproductive task, it was one of the principles upon which a Matherly had founded the publishing house over a century ago. Noah could mock their archaic traditions because he hadn't been born a Matherly. He was a member of the family by marriage, not blood, and that was a significant difference that explained his more relaxed attitude toward tradition.

A Matherly's blood was tinted with ink. An appreciation for it seemed to flow through the family's veins. Maris firmly believed that her family's admiration and respect for the written word and for writers had been fundamental to their success and longevity as publishers.

"I got an advance copy of the article," Noah said.

She picked up the magazine he'd carried in with him. A Post-It marked a specific page. Turning to it, she said, "Ah, great photo."

"Good photographer."

"Good subject."

"Thank you."

" 'Noah Reed is forty, but could pass for much younger,' " she read aloud from the article. Angling her head back, she gave him a critical look. "I agree. You don't look a day over thirty-nine."

"Ha-ha."

" 'Daily workouts in the Matherly Press gym on the sixth floor—one of Reed's innovations when he joined the firm three years ago—keeps all six feet of him lean and supple.' Well, this writer is certainly enamored. Did you ever have a thing with her?"

He chuckled. "Absolutely not."

"She's one of the few."

On their wedding day, Maris had teasingly remarked to him that so many single women were mourning the loss of one of the city's most eligible bachelors, she was surprised that the doors of St. Patrick's Cathedral weren't draped in black crepe. "Does she get around to mentioning your business acumen and the contributions you've made to Matherly Press?"

"Farther down."

"Let's see . . . 'graying at the temples, which adds to his distinguished good looks' . . . So on and so forth about your commanding demeanor and charm. Are you sure— Oh, here's something. 'He shares the helm at Matherly Press with his father-in-law, publishing legend Daniel Matherly, who serves as chairman and CEO, and Reed's wife, Maris Matherly-Reed, whom he claims has perfect selection and editorial skills. He modestly credits her with the company's reputation for publishing best-sellers.'" Pleased, she smiled up at him. "Did you say that?"

"And more that she didn't include."

"Then thank you very much."

"I only said what I know to be true."

Maris read the remainder of the flattering article, then set the magazine aside. "Very nice. But for all her ga-ga-ness she overlooked two major biographical points."

"And they are?"

"That you're also an excellent writer."

"*The Vanquished* is old news."

"But it should be mentioned anytime your name appears in print."

"What's the second thing?" he asked in the brusque tone he used whenever she brought up his one and only published novel.

"She said nothing about your marvelous massage techniques."

"Happy to oblige."

Closing her eyes, Maris tilted her head to one side. "A little lower on your . . . Ahh. There." He dug his strong thumb into a spot between her scapulas, and the tension began to dissolve.

"You're in knots," he said. "Serves you right for scavenging through that heap of garbage all day."

"As it turns out, it might not have been time wasted. I actually found something that sparked my interest."

"You're joking."

"No."

"Fiction or non?"

"Fiction. Only a prologue, but it's intriguing. It starts—"

"I want to hear all about it, darling. But you really should shake a leg if we're going to get there in time."

He dropped a kiss on the top of her head, then tried to withdraw. But Maris reached for his hands and pulled them over her shoulders, holding them flattened against her chest. "Is tonight mandatory?"

"More or less."

"We could miss one function, couldn't we? Dad begged off tonight."

"That's why we should be there. Matherly Press bought a table. Two empty seats would be noticeable. One of our authors is receiving an award."

"His agent and editor are attending with him. He won't be without a cheering section." She pulled his hands down onto her breasts. "Let's call in sick. Go home and shut out the world. Open a bottle of wine, the cheaper the better. Get in the Jacuzzi and feed each other a pizza. Make love in some room other than the bedroom. Maybe even two rooms."

Laughing, he squeezed her breasts affectionately. "What did you say this prologue was about?" He pulled his hands from beneath hers and headed for the door.

Maris groaned with disappointment. "I thought I was making you an offer you couldn't refuse."

"Tempting. Very. But if we're not at this dinner, it'll arouse suspicion."

"You're right. I'd hate for people to think that we're still acting like newlyweds who crave evenings alone."

"Which is true."

"But . . . ?"

"But we also have professional responsibilities, Maris. As you are well aware. It's important for industry insiders to know that when they refer to Matherly Press, it damn well better be in either the present or future tense, not the past tense."

"And that's why we attend nearly every publishing event held in New York," she said as though it were part of a memorized catechism.

"Precisely."

Their calendars were filled with breakfasts, luncheons, dinners, receptions, and cocktail parties. Noah believed it was extremely important, virtually compulsory, that they be seen as active participants within literary circles, especially since her father could no longer be involved to the extent he once had been.

Recently Daniel Matherly had slowed down. He didn't attend as many insider gatherings. He was no longer accepting speaking engagements, although the requests still poured in. The Four Seasons was calling daily now to inquire if Daniel would be using his reserved table for lunch or if they were free to seat another party there.

For almost five decades, Daniel had been a force to be reckoned with. Under his leadership, Matherly Press had set the industry standards, dictated trends, dominated the bestseller lists. His name had become synonymous with book publishing both domestically and in foreign markets. He had been a juggernaut who, over a period of months, had voluntarily been decreasing his momentum.

However, his semi-retirement did not spell the end, or even a weakening, of the publishing house's viability. Noah thought it was vitally important that the book publishing community understand that. If that meant going to award dinners several times a month, that's what they would do.

He checked his wristwatch. "How much time do you need? I should let the driver know when we'll be downstairs."

Maris sighed with resignation. "Give me twenty minutes."

"I'll be generous. Take thirty." He blew her a kiss before leaving.

But Maris didn't plunge into her overhaul right away. Instead, she asked her assistant to place a call. She'd had another idea on how she might track down the author of *Envy*.

While waiting for the requested call to be placed, she gazed out her office windows. Extending nearly from floor to ceiling, they formed a corner of the room, providing her a southeastern exposure. Midtown Manhattan was experiencing a mild summer evening. The sun had slipped behind the skyscrapers, casting a premature twilight on the streets below. Already lights were coming on inside buildings, making the brick and granite structures appear to twinkle. Through the windows of neighboring buildings, Maris could see other professionals wrapping up for the day.

The avenues were jammed with competing after-work and pretheater traffic. Taxies vied for inches of space, nosing themselves into impossibly small channels between buses and delivery trucks. Couriers on bicycles, seemingly with death wishes, perilously played chicken with motor traffic. Revolving doors disgorged pedestrians onto the crowded sidewalks, where they jostled for space and wielded briefcases and shopping bags like weapons.

Across Avenue of the Americas, a queue was forming outside Radio City Music Hall, where Tony Bennett was performing this evening. She, Noah, and her father had been offered complimentary VIP tickets, but they'd had to decline them because of the literary award banquet.

Which she should be dressing for, she reminded herself, just as her telephone beeped. "He's on line one," her assistant informed her.

"Thanks. You don't need to wait. See you tomorrow." Maris depressed the blinking button. "Hello?"

"Yeah. Deputy Dwight Harris here."

"Hello, Deputy Harris. Thank you for taking my call. My name is Maris Matherly-Reed."

"Say again?"

She did.

"Uh-huh."

Maris paused, giving him time to comment or ask a question, but he didn't, so she went straight to the reason for the call. "I'm trying to reach someone, an individual who I believe lives on St. Anne Island."

"That's in our county."

"Georgia, correct?"

"Yes, ma'am," he proudly replied.

"Is St. Anne actually an island?"

"Not much o' one. What I mean is, it's small. But it's an island, awright. Little less than two miles out from the mainland. Who're you looking for?"

"Someone with the initials P.M.E."

"Did you say P.M.E.?"

"Have you ever heard of anyone who goes by those initials?"

"Can't say that I have, ma'am. We talking about a man or woman?"

"Unfortunately, I don't know."

"You don't know. Huh." After a beat or two, the deputy asked, "If you don't even know if it's a man or woman, what do you want with 'em?"

"It's business."

"Business."

"That's right."

"Huh."

Dead end. Maris tried again. "I thought you might know, or might have heard of someone who—"

"Nope."

This was going nowhere and her allotted time was running out. "Well, thank you for your time, Deputy Harris. I'm sorry to have bothered you."

"No bother."

"Would you mind taking down my name and numbers? Then if you think of something or hear of someone with these initials, I would appreciate being notified."

After she gave him her telephone numbers, he said, "Say, ma'am? If it's back child support or an outstanding arrest warrant or something like 'at, I'd be happy to see if—"

"No, no. It's not a legal matter in any sense."

"Business."

"That's right."

"Well, okay, then," he said with noticeable disappointment. "Sorry I couldn't he'p you."

She thanked him again, then closed her office and hurried

down the hallway to the ladies' room, where her cocktail dress had been hanging since she'd arrived for work early that morning. Because she frequently changed from business to evening attire before leaving the building, she kept a full complement of toiletries and cosmetics in a locker. She put them to use now.

When she joined Noah at the elevator fifteen minutes later, he gave a long wolf whistle, then kissed her cheek. "Nice turnaround. A miracle, actually. You look fantastic."

As they descended to street level, she assessed her reflection in the metal elevator door and realized that her efforts hadn't been in vain. "Fantastic," was a slight exaggeration, but considering the dishevelment she'd started with, she looked better than she had any right to expect.

She'd chosen to wear a cranberry-colored silk sheath with narrow straps and a scooped neckline. Her nod toward evening glitter came in the form of diamond studs in her ears and a crystal-encrusted Judith Leiber handbag in the shape of a butterfly, a Christmas gift from her father. She was carrying a pashmina shawl purchased in Paris during a side trip there following the international book fair in Frankfurt.

She had gathered her shoulder-length hair into a sleek, low ponytail. The hairdo looked chic and sophisticated rather than desperate, which had been the case. She had retouched her eye makeup, outlined her lips with a pencil, and filled them in with gloss. To give color to her fluorescent-light pallor, she had applied powdered bronzer to her cheeks, chin, forehead, and décolletage. Her push-up bra, an engineering marvel, had created a flattering cleavage that filled up the neckline of her dress.

"'Her tan and tits were store-bought.'"

The elevator doors opened onto the ground floor. Noah looked at her curiously as he stepped aside to let her exit ahead of him. "I beg your pardon?"

She laughed softly. "Nothing. Just quoting something I read today."

CHAPTER 2

Although it had stopped raining a half hour earlier, the air was already so moisture-laden the rainwater couldn't evaporate. It collected in puddles. It beaded on flowers' petals and the fuzz of ripe peaches ready to be picked. The limbs of evergreens were bowed under the additional weight. Fat drops rolled off hardwood leaves recently washed clean and splashed onto the spongy, saturated ground.

The slightest breeze would have shaken water from the trees, creating miniature rain showers, but there was scarcely any movement of air. The atmosphere was inert and had a texture almost as compacted as the silence.

Deputy Dwight Harris alighted from the golf cart he had borrowed at the St. Anne landing. Before starting up the pathway to the house, he removed his hat and paused, telling himself that he needed a moment to get his bearings, when what he was actually doing was second-guessing his decision to come here alone after sundown. He didn't quite know what to expect.

He'd never been here before, although he knew about this house, awright. Anybody who was ever on St. Anne Island had heard stories about the plantation house at the easternmost tip of the island, situated on a little finger of land that pointed out toward Africa. Some of the tales he'd heard about the place stretched credibility. But the descriptions of the house were, by God, damn near accurate.

Typical of colonial Low Country architecture, the two-story white frame house was sitting on top of an aged brick basement. Six broad steps led up to the deep veranda that extended all the way across the front of the house and wrapped around both sides. The front door had been painted a glossy black, as had all the hurricane shutters that flanked the windows on both stories. Six smooth columns supported the second-floor balcony. Twin chimneys acted like bookends against the steeply pitched roof. It looked pretty much like Deputy Harris had imagined it would.

He hadn't counted on it looking so spooky, is all.

He jumped and uttered a soft exclamation of fright when a raindrop landed on the back of his neck with a hard splat. It had dripped from a low-hanging branch of the tree under which he was standing. Wiping the wetness away, he replaced his hat and glanced around to make sure no one had seen his nervous reaction. It was the gathering dusk and the inclement weather that was giving the place an eerie feel. Cursing himself for behaving like a coward, he forced his feet into motion.

Dodging puddles, he made his way up the crushed-shell path, which was lined by twin rows of live oaks, four to a side. Spanish moss hung from the branches in trailing bunches. The roots of the ancient trees snaked along the ground, some of them as thick as a fat man's thigh.

Altogether, it was an impressive front entry. Majestic, you might say. The back of the house, Harris knew, overlooked the Atlantic.

The house hadn't started out this grand. The four original rooms had been built more than two centuries ago by the planter who'd bought the island from a colonist who decided he preferred dying of old age in England to succumbing to yellow fever in the newly founded American nation. The house had expanded with the plantation's success, first with indigo and sugar cane, then with cotton.

Several generations into the dynasty, those first four rooms were converted into slave quarters, and construction of the big house was begun. In its day, it was a marvel, at least for St. Anne Island. Building materials and all the furnishings had been shipped in, then dragged on sleds pulled by mules through dense forests and fertile fields to the home site. It had taken years to complete, but it had been sturdily constructed, withstanding Union army occupation and the lashings of a couple dozen hurricanes.

Then it succumbed to a bug.

Around the beginning of the twentieth century, the boll weevil ruined more than the cotton crop. More damaging than weather and war, the boll weevil crushed the local economy and destroyed life as it had been lived on St. Anne.

A descendant of the plantation's original owner had correctly forecast his imminent doom and hanged himself on the dining room chandelier. The rest of the family stole off the island in the middle of the night, never to be heard of again, leaving debts and unpaid taxes.

Decades passed. The forest eventually reclaimed the property surrounding the house, just as it did the fields once white with cotton. Varmints occupied rooms once inhabited by aristocracy and visited by one United States president. The only people to ever venture inside the dilapidated mansion were crazy kids accepting a dare or an occasional drunk looking for a place to sleep it off.

It remained in ruin until a little over a year ago when an outsider, not an islander, bought it and commenced a massive renovation. Harris figured he was probably a northerner who'd seen *Gone With the Wind* several times and wanted himself an antebellum mansion on southern soil, a Yankee with more money than good sense.

Word around the island, though, was positive about the new owner. He'd made noticeable improvements on the place, folks said. But in Harris's opinion there was still a lot to be done if it was going to shine as it had in its heyday. The deputy didn't envy the new owner the monumental task or the expense involved in such an undertaking. Nor was he envious of the bad luck that seemed to go hand in glove with this place.

Legend had it that the hanged man's ghost still resided in the old house and that the dining room chandelier swung from the ceiling for no reason that anybody could detect.

Harris didn't put much stock in ghost stories. He'd seen flesh-and-blood people do much scarier stuff than any mischief a ghost could drum up. Even so, he would have welcomed a little more illumination as he mounted the steps, crossed the veranda, and approached the front door.

He tapped the brass knocker tentatively, then harder. Seconds ticked by as ponderously as rain dripped from the eaves. It wasn't that late, but maybe the resident was already in bed. Country folk tended to turn in earlier than city dwellers, didn't they?

Harris considered leaving and coming back some other time—preferably before the sun went down. But then he heard approaching footsteps. Seconds later the front door was pulled open from the inside—but not by much.

"Yes?"

Harris peered into the crack formed by the open door. He had psyched himself up to expect anything from the hanging ghost to the twin barrels of a sawed-off shotgun aimed at his belly by a disgruntled homeowner that he'd unnecessarily dragged out of bed.

Thankfully he was greeted by neither, and the man seemed reasonably friendly. Harris couldn't see him well and the features of his face blended into the shadows behind him, but his voice sounded pleasant enough. At least he hadn't cussed him. Yet.

"Evenin', sir. I'm Deputy Dwight Harris. From the sheriff's office over in Savannah."

The man leaned forward slightly and glanced past him toward the golf cart parked at the end of the path. To discourage tourism and unwelcome visitors to the island, there wasn't a ferry to St. Anne from the mainland. Anyone coming here came by a boat they either owned or chartered. When they arrived, they either walked or rented a golf cart to get around the island's nine thousand acres, give or take a few hundred. Only permanent residents drove cars on the narrow roads, many of which had been left unpaved on purpose.

The golf cart wasn't as official-looking as a squad car, and Harris figured it diminished his authority a bit. To stoke his self-confidence, he hiked up his slipping gun belt.

The man behind the door asked, "How can I help you, Deputy Harris?"

"First off, I apologize for disturbing you. But I got a call earlier this evening. From a gal up in New York." The man waited him out, saying nothing. "Said she was trying to track down somebody who goes by the initials P.M.E."

"Really?"

"That's what she said. I didn't let on like the name registered with me."

"Did it?"

"Register, you mean? No, sir. Can't rightly say it did."

"Nevertheless, you're here."

"I'll admit she got my curiosity up. Never knew anybody to go only by his initials, you see. Don't worry, though. 'Round here, we respect a person's privacy."

"An admirable practice."

"St. Anne has a history of folks hiding out on her for one reason or another."

The moment it was out, Harris wished he hadn't said it. It smacked of an accusation of some sort. A long silence ensued. He cleared his throat nervously before continuing. "So anyhow,